THE FIREPLUG
IS FIRST BASE

by P. J. Petersen
and Betsy James

PUFFIN BOOKS

For my brothers—Carl, John, Jerry, and Ed—
who played ball with me.

P.J.P.

This book is for Jemez!

B.J.

PUFFIN BOOKS
Published by the Penguin Group
Penguin Putnam Inc., 375 Hudson Street, New York, New York 10014, U.S.A.
Penguin Books Ltd, 27 Wrights Lane, London W8 5TZ, England
Penguin Books Australia Ltd, Ringwood, Victoria, Australia
Penguin Books Canada Ltd, 10 Alcorn Avenue, Toronto, Ontario, Canada M4V 3B2
Penguin Books (N.Z.) Ltd, 182-190 Wairau Road, Auckland 10, New Zealand

Penguin Books Ltd, Registered Offices: Harmondsworth, Middlesex, England

First published in the United States of America by Dutton Children's Books,
a division of Penguin Books USA Inc., 1990
Published in Puffin Books, 1992
Reissued 1998

1 3 5 7 9 10 8 6 4 2

THE LIBRARY OF CONGRESS HAS CATALOGED THE PREVIOUS PUFFIN EDITION AS FOLLOWS:
Petersen, P. J.
The fireplug is first base / by P. J. Petersen and Betsy James
p. cm.
Summary: A small baseball player surprises his bigger teammates when
he finally gets his chance at bat.
ISBN 0-14-036165-0
[1. Baseball—Fiction. 2. Size—Fiction.] I. James, Betsy. II. Title.
[PZ7.P44197Fi 1992] [Fic]—dc20 92-18956

This edition ISBN 0-14-130056-6

Printed in the United States of America

RL: 1.9

OTHER CHAPTER BOOKS FROM PUFFIN

The Four-Legged Ghosts   Hoffman/Seeley

The Gadget War   Duffey/Wilson

Hey, New Kid!   Duffey/Thompson

Horrible Harry in Room 2B   Kline/Remkiewicz

I Hate Camping   Petersen/Remkiewicz

I Hate Company   Petersen/James

The Math Wiz   Duffey/Wilson

Rats on the Range   James Marshall

Russell Rides Again   Hurwitz/Hoban

Sasha and the Wolfcub   Jungman/Wright

The Sub   Petersen/Johnson

Wackysaurus: Dinosaur Jokes   Phillips/Barrett

The William Problem   Baker/Iosa

1 · Time for Baseball

I was out in front of our building, waiting for my friend Tank. We were going to play ball. My little brother Flea was with me, jumping up and down.

PLEASE, Joe, can I bat today?

That's why we call him Flea—because he's little and jumps around.

In our ball games, the little kids don't bat. They just play catcher or fielder the whole time.

"Come on, Joe. I want to be a regular player," said Flea.

3

Just then, Tank came out of his building. His real name is Clyde, but nobody calls him that except his mother.

He swung his arms like he was hitting a home run.

We always play ball on Pine Street.
That's where our friend Tony lives,
and he has the only bat.

Tank, can I bat today?

You can be catcher.

"I don't want to be catcher.
The catcher just runs after the
ball," said Flea.

"That's a good job for a little kid," Tank
said.

I'm not so little. I want to be a regular player.

I want to bat!

We'll see.

Tank started down the sidewalk.
Flea stayed where he was.

That's what you always say. Then you never let me bat!

Maybe this will be your lucky day.

Flea didn't move.

"He has to come," I told Tank. "Mom says I have to watch him."

"I don't need a baby-sitter," Flea said.

"I know it," I said. "But you do need somebody to help you stand on your head, don't you?"

"And you need somebody to show you
how to make paper airplanes, don't you?"

"And you need somebody to help you
draw pictures of trucks, don't you?"

"Then you'd better come play ball the way we say, or I won't do any of those things."

2 · Getting Started

Pine Street is a good place to play ball.
Not many drivers come that way,
and cars can only park on
one side of the
street.

When we got there,
Tony was already
hitting fly balls

to his little brother Matt

and his little sister Mary.

They missed the ball every time. We
use an old soft tennis ball that won't
break windows—we hope.

"You two can be fielders for both teams," Tank said. "Just like always."

"I'm tired of that," Matt said. "We just chase the ball, and we never get to bat."

Tony threw me the ball.

"Toss it here, Joe," Flea yelled. He was trying to act like one of the regular players.

We can be a team, Joe!

You and I can play Tank and Tony.

"Baker will be here right away," Tank said. "He and Joe will play Tony and me—just like always."

TANK'S TEAM

JOE'S TEAM

TANK AND TONY

JOE AND BAKER

BUT... FLEA, MARY, AND MATT

HAVE TO PLAY ON BOTH TEAMS—
JUST LIKE ALWAYS.

Tony went into the alley and came back with the lid of a garbage can.

Here's home plate.

CLANK

Just then Baker came
down Pine Street with
his dog on a leash.

"You can play ball first, then walk the dog," Tank told Baker.

"OK," said Baker. "I guess I can play for a while."

"Maybe you'd better not," Flea said. "What if your mother saw you playing ball when you were supposed to be walking the dog?"

To see which team batted first, Tank leaned the garbage can lid against a parking meter. "All right," he said. "The first one to hit the lid bats first."

Tank blew on the ball and threw it, but it sailed over the lid.

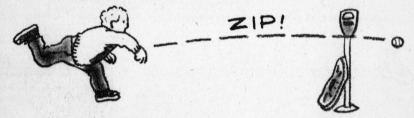

ZIP!

Baker missed too.

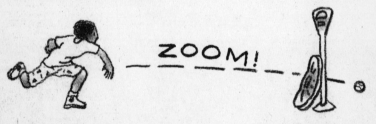

ZOOM!

Then Tony hit the lid,

BWANG.

so Tony and Tank got to bat first.

3 · Batter Up

Baker kept throwing
the ball over the
batter's head.

And Flea kept running
after the ball.

When Baker pitched the ball close to
the plate, Tony and Tank smashed the ball
and ran around the bases for home runs.

Sometimes Tony ran around the bases
two times.

In our games, when a team makes one out, the other team gets to bat. But that day, getting even one person out seemed impossible.

Tony and Tank scored

22 RUNS.

That wasn't enough for Tank. He pounded the bat on the garbage can lid.

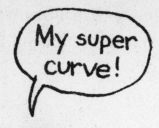

Tank hit the ball far up the street.

The ball bounced off a
lamppost and kept rolling.
Matt ran after the ball while
Tank trotted around the bases.

BOINK

Go
for it,
Tank!

When Tank stepped on home plate, he looked up the street and started to run again—faster this time.

Matt grabbed the ball and started running back toward us.

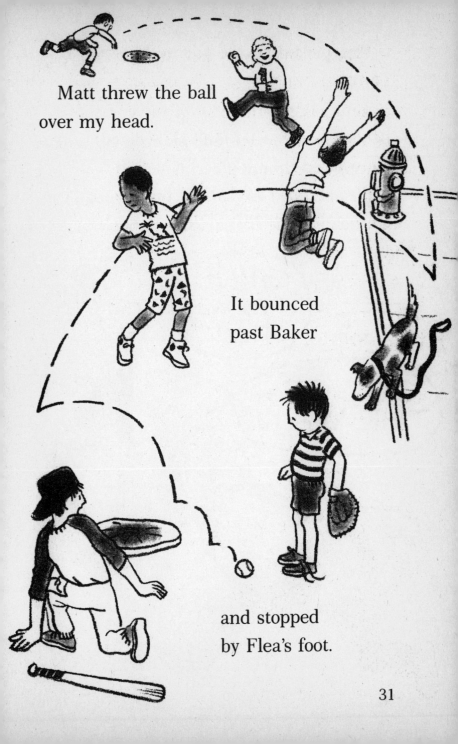

Matt threw the ball
over my head.

It bounced
past Baker

and stopped
by Flea's foot.

31

Flea picked up the ball and looked at
Tank.

Tank tagged the door of the car and
headed home. He didn't slow down at all.
He wanted that double home run.

Flea stepped in front of the garbage can
lid, holding the ball in both hands.

Flea stood still, and . . .

Flea flew into the air. He came down on his back, but he kept hold of the ball.

"We'll see," Tank said.

4 · Flea at Bat

Tank pitched for his team. Tony played first base. He petted Baker's dog while he waited for us to hit.

Baker hit a double, and I hit the ball under a truck for a home run.

Now it's my turn.

"It's not fair," Baker said. "If you want him to bat, let him bat when your team's up."

Don't make trouble, Baker. It's OK with the rest of your team.

Baker looked at me. "What do you mean the rest of my team? Joe's the rest of the team."

"Then let Joe decide," Tank said.

Come on, Joe!

I'll do the dishes tonight!

"Just meet the ball with your bat," I said. "Don't try to kill it."

"Easy out," Tony said. He moved up close, and Baker's dog came with him.

Somebody had to play catcher, so I got down behind the lid.

Tank threw the ball.

Flea swung and missed it by a foot.
Tank threw the ball again.

Flea missed it
by two feet.

Tank blew on the ball. "All right, here comes strike three."

Tank pitched the ball.

The ball rolled two feet.

"Oh, yeah," Flea said. He dropped
the bat and took off for the fireplug.

Tony ran to get the ball.
So did Baker's dog.

The dog got there first.

The dog ran into the alley, and Tony went after it.

Two seconds later, a big orange cat raced out of the alley and headed for a lamppost. Baker's dog was right behind it, with the ball still in his mouth.

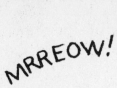

MRREOW!

RRREOW!

PF.SSST!

The cat ran up
the pole. Baker's
dog opened its
mouth to bark,
and
the ball
bounced
into
the street.

ARF!

ARF!

ARF!

By then, Flea was stepping on home plate.

Flea didn't stop. He headed for the fireplug again.

The ball rolled toward some girls who were jumping rope.

Tony tripped over the jump rope.
One girl threw the ball
toward Matt.

It went over his head.

Flea tagged the fireplug and
headed for the manhole cover.

The ball hit the ground and bounced
into the shopping bag of a woman who
was walking by.

Matt ran up to her and reached into the
bag.

The woman
took out a
package of
cookies.

"Throw the ball!" Tony shouted.
Flea stepped on the garbage can lid.

Matt took a cookie from the woman.

"Throw the ball!" Tony yelled to him.
"Hurry!"

Matt took a bite of the cookie, then threw the ball as hard as he could. It sailed high over Tony's head and landed on the awning in front of the secondhand store.

Flea stepped on the
manhole cover. He
was laughing by
then and just
jogging along.

Mary ran up. She
handed Tony a broom
that was leaning
against the store.

Knock
it down!

53

Flea tagged the door of the Ford and
ran for home. He still had time to make it.

"Throw me the ball, Tony!" Tank yelled.
He stepped in front of the garbage can lid.
He wasn't going to let Flea go past him
and touch the plate.

Tony threw the ball toward home.

Tank smiled and crouched down.

Flea lowered his head and put his
hands in front of him.

Tank looked like a wall.

Flea didn't slow down.

I stood back and held my breath.

When Flea was one step in front of
Tank, he jumped up and dove
right over Tank's head.

Flea slid down Tank's back and landed
on top of the lid.

Tank caught the ball, but it was too
late.

57

Right then, Tony's mother called him
and Matt and Mary for dinner.

Tank and Flea and I walked back home.